This Book belongs to

To every kid with a big imagination
-B.W.

Vegetable Soup: A Pretend Story by Bola Williams

Illustrated by Jas Chen

Text & Illustration copyright © 2020 by Bola Williams

Pears lane Publishing is an imprint of Blue Thread, LLC

Visit www.pearslanepublishing.com

Printed in U.S.A

ISBN 978-1-7344484-3-6 (print)

ISBN 978-1-7344484-4-3 (Ebook)

Vegetable Soup
A Pretend Story

Written by
BOLA WILLIAMS

Illustrated by
JAS CHEN

Pears Lane Publishing
New York

Bailey is happy to be at school today.
In a circle with friends, she's ready to play.

The teacher smiles, "What a happy little group. Would you like to make some pretend soup?"

Hands in the air, everyone cheers,

"WOOO!"

Bailey is super excited too!

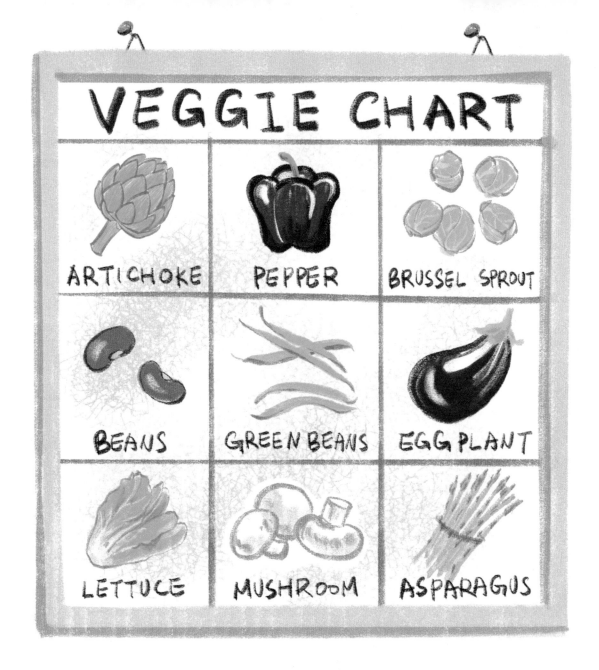

"Let's each choose a vegetable!" the teacher explains.
"We can imagine anything when we use our brains."

Bailey thinks playing pretend soup will be fun.
She knows which vegetable is her favorite one.

Carter says, "I'm a CARROT. They have crazy hair! Growing wild here and there and everywhere!"

"Can I be a GREEN PEA?" giggles cute playful Penny.
"When peas run and roll they look really funny!"

MMM, MMM, MMM!

"I want to be a POTATO!" declares little Pete. "They have silly eyes and sometimes they're sweet!"

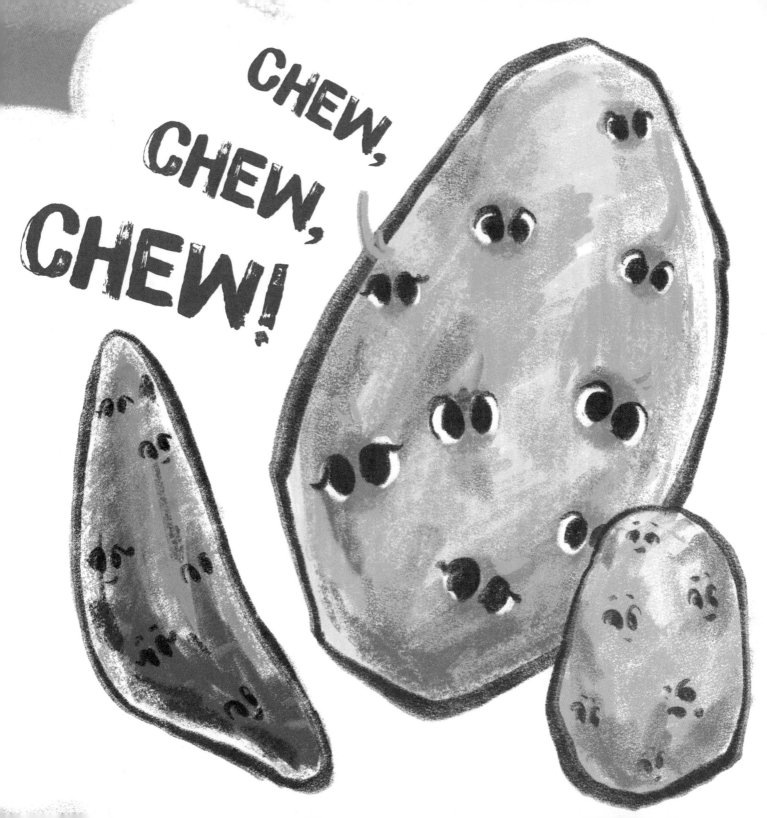

"I can pretend to be CORN." whispers shy sweet Caitlin. "They have lots of friends and a green blanket to play in."

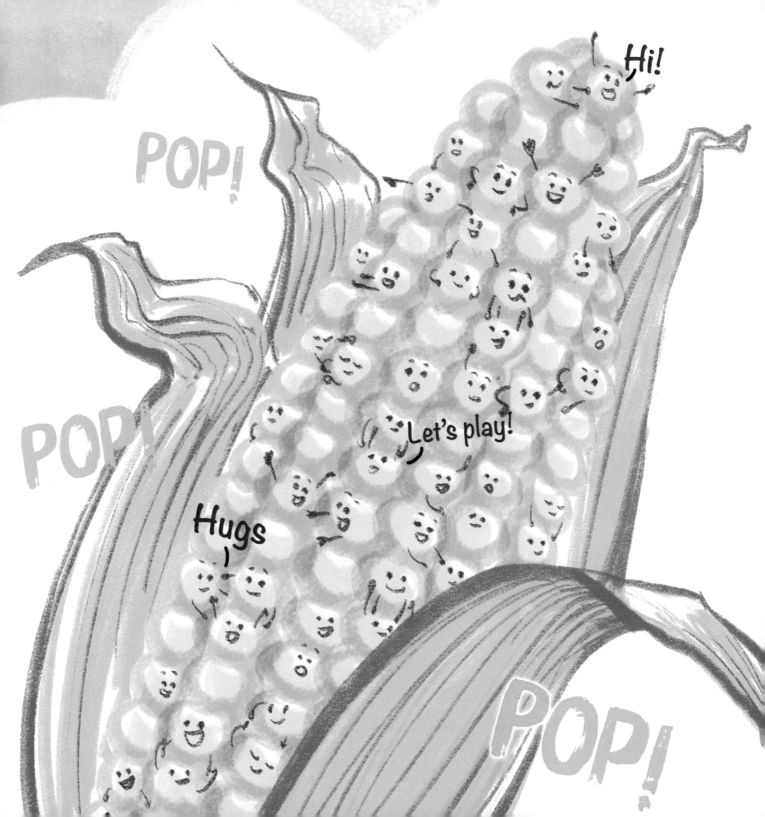

"I'll be a TOMATO!" exclaims jolly Tommy. "They're ripe and juicy when the sun's really sunny."

Sam shares, "I'll be CELERY, with lines like tracks! Engine choo-choo trains ride along the cracks!"

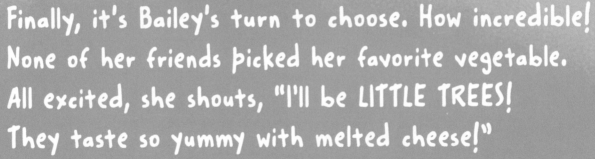

Finally, it's Bailey's turn to choose. How incredible!
None of her friends picked her favorite vegetable.
All excited, she shouts, "I'll be LITTLE TREES!
They taste so yummy with melted cheese!"

But Wait... little trees? That sounds very silly. Her friends giggle aloud and one said

"really?"

"Oh, no!" thought Bailey, "This can't be good. They must know littles trees are real food." Bailey is quite confused and oh, so sad. If she could be at home, she'd be so glad.

"It is a vegetable!" declares Bailey. "Mom made some last night!" She remembers that it tasted so good she ate every bite.

"Little trees have LOTS of tiny leaves." explains Bailey.
"Sprouting all on top, I think they must grow daily."

florets

"They have a trunk that makes them really, really tall. If you cut their trunk that makes them really, really small."

"At the grocery store in the vegetable bin, little trees are next to little white trees but they're GREEN."

"That sounds like broccoli" says the teacher to Bailey's delight.

"Bro-cco-li?" asks Bailey as she scrunches her eyes up real tight.
"Oh, yes! BROCCOLI! I call them little trees. When I look at broccoli, a tree is what I see.

Bailey jumps into the circle with her group. They wiggle and jiggle to mix their pretend soup.

Now, she's excited again and her friends are happy too!

It's your turn to pretend so, which vegetable are you?

Made in the USA
Las Vegas, NV
02 November 2021